# The Great Carrot Caper!

**EGMONT**

*We bring stories to life*

First published in Great Britain 2015 by Egmont UK Limited
The Yellow Building, 1 Nicholas Road, London W11 4AN

© Masha and the Bear Ltd. 2008-2015
www.mashabear.com

Series created by: Oleg Kuzovkov. Art Director: Ilya Trusov.

ISBN 978 1 4052 7717 4
59702/2
Printed in Italy

MIX
Paper from
responsible sources
FSC® C018306
FSC
www.fsc.org

It was springtime at last! Bear skipped outside to his garden.

But what should he plant? Masha had an idea. "Let's plant carrots!" she said.

So Bear planted the seeds and watered them carefully.

Carrots

Bear worked very hard in his garden.
Every day, he measured the carrots.
They grew bigger and bigger.

Bear dreamed of growing the most
enormous carrots in the world!

But one morning, someone hopped into the garden to pick the carrots. Someone small and furry ...

It was Rabbit!

"**GRRR**," grumbled Bear.

He picked up Rabbit and took him outside the gate.

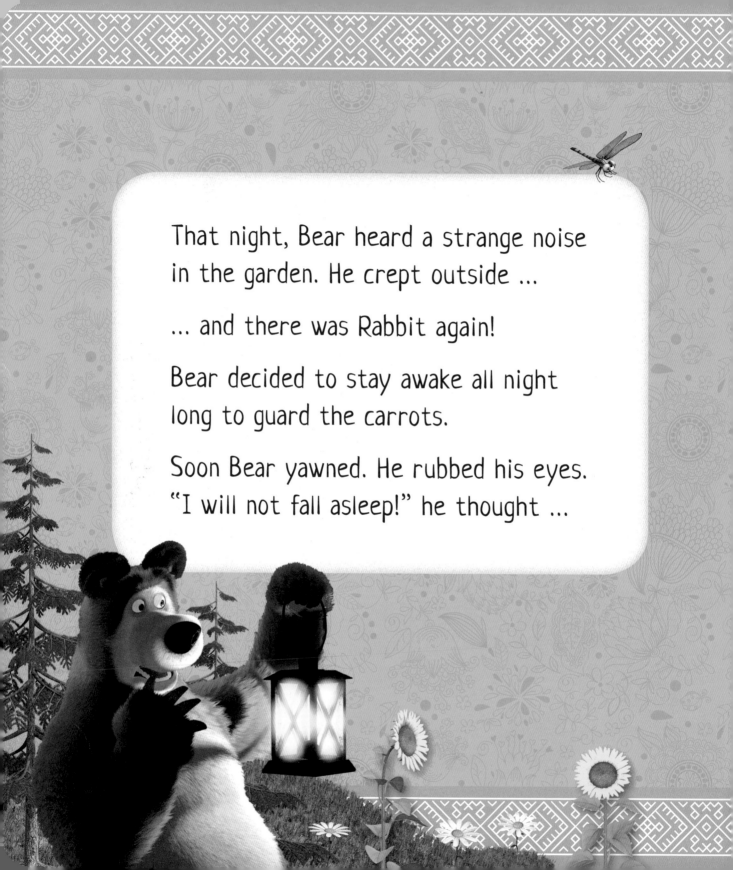

That night, Bear heard a strange noise in the garden. He crept outside ...

... and there was Rabbit again!

Bear decided to stay awake all night long to guard the carrots.

Soon Bear yawned. He rubbed his eyes. "I will not fall asleep!" he thought ...

**Z**z**z**z**z**z**! Bear fell fast asleep!

He slept so soundly, he didn't notice someone hopping past. Someone small and furry, who liked eating big, juicy carrots ...

Masha arrived in the morning, but it was too late. Rabbit had finished his carrot feast!

"Now I'm going to catch you," laughed Masha, as she grabbed for a net.

Masha chased Rabbit round and round the garden, through the trees, and past the bees, until ...

**CRASH!** The beehives toppled over. The bees flew straight for Bear. Bear woke up. "**RAAARRRGH!**" he howled.

Rabbit ran inside.

Masha chased Rabbit around and around the house, up the stairs, and over the chairs, until ...

**SMASH!** A bookcase came crashing down.

**"RAAARRRGH!"** Bear roared.

Rabbit scurried away. Bear's home was **a mess!**

"I didn't catch him," Masha said. "Maybe he'll come back and I can chase him **again!**"

But Bear had a better idea ...

Bear painted big pictures of Masha and put them all over the garden.

That night, Rabbit crawled under the fence. He tiptoed into the garden ... and something that looked just like Masha was waiting for him!

Rabbit dashed away as quickly as his legs could carry him.

Bear laughed and laughed and laughed.

And now Bear's garden is finally full of big, juicy carrots!